WITHDRAWN

For more than forty years,
Yearling has been the leading name
in classic and award-winning literature
for young readers.

Yearling books feature children's
favorite authors and characters,
providing dynamic stories of adventure,
humor, history, mystery, and fantasy.

Trust Yearling paperbacks to entertain,
inspire, and promote the love of reading
in all children.

Don't miss these groovy books!

Little Genie

Little Genie
Home on the Range

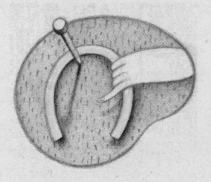

MIRANDA JONES

illustrated by David Calver

A YEARLING BOOK

Published by Yearling, an imprint of Random House Children's Books
a division of Random House, Inc., New York

This is a work of fiction. Names, characters, places, and incidents either are the
product of the author's imagination or are used fictitiously. Any resemblance to
actual persons, living or dead, events, or locales is entirely coincidental.

Text copyright © 2008 by Working Partners Ltd.
Illustrations copyright © 2008 by David Calver

A Working Partners Book

Visit us on the Web! www.randomhouse.com/kids

Educators and librarians, for a variety of teaching tools, visit us at
www.randomhouse.com/teachers

Library of Congress Cataloging-in-Publication Data
Jones, Miranda.
Home on the range / by Miranda Jones ; illustrated by David Calver.
p. cm.—(Little Genie)
Summary: When Ali wishes for the family vacation to be more fun, she gets
more than she bargained for when the spa is turned into a Wild West ranch,
cactus start walking, and a mule starts talking.
ISBN 978-0-440-42226-6 (trade pbk.)—ISBN 978-0-385-90532-9 (lib. bdg.)
[1. Genies—Fiction. 2. Magic—Fiction. 3. Wishes—Fiction. 4. Ranch life—
Fiction.] I. Calver, David, ill. II. Title.
PZ7.J7237Ho 2008
[Fic]—dc22   2007003181

Printed in the United States of America

April 2008

10 9 8 7 6 5 4 3 2 1

Special thanks to Narinder Dhami

Contents

Chapter One
Do the Math!

This is just great! My best friend, Mary, invited me to go swimming with her family at Great Barrier Reef this weekend. I LOVE GBR!!! It's this cool water park with all kinds of tubes and slides and an amazing wave pool. And not only that, her mom and dad said they'd take us out for pizza, too!

But guess what?

I can't go.

Instead, Mom, Dad, Gran, Bulldozer (aka my annoying little brother, Jake), and I are spending the weekend at Joseph West's Relaxation Retreat. It's this fancy luxury spa. Mom got a last-minute reservation. She says it's going to help us "recharge and relax as a family."

How could *anywhere* with Bulldozer be relaxing?

Do the math! Jake + vacation = big trouble.

And to top it all off, there's Little Genie. She's upset because she wants to come with us but I'm not so sure she should.

Jake + Genie + vacation = bigger trouble!

I hate to see Genie so sad, though. She was so gloomy when she was helping me pack. To be honest, I'd take a vacation with Genie over one with Bulldozer any day. At least Genie's cool and cute. Unlike some people, who are nicknamed after construction equipment.

But if Genie came with us, her magic might start going wrong again. We might get swamped by a tidal wave (no joke, that actually happened), or a purple tiger might appear again or something. How would I explain *that* to my family? They might find out about Little Genie.

But no one else can *ever* find out about her, because then she'd be stuck inside her lamp forever and lose all her magic powers. And I can't risk that by bringing her with me.

Don't get me wrong, it's the biggest fun *ever* having my very own genie and getting three wishes every time the sand in Genie's watch starts to run through the hourglass.

But I never know what's going to happen next!

Chapter Two
Genie or No Genie?

Dinner? Check. Homework? Check. Shower? Check.

Ali Miller jogged down the stairs. At last, free time! She couldn't wait to watch her favorite game show, *Stay or Go*. But as she reached the bottom of the steps, she frowned. The TV was in the living room. And there were some *really* strange noises coming from the living room.

"Breathe!" Ali's mom was drifting around

the room wrapped in a fluffy pink bathrobe and wearing an eye mask. She was breathing extremely loudly. "In . . . out . . . in . . . out . . . *relax.*"

"Mom, be careful!" Ali cried as her mother almost crashed into the TV.

Mom lifted her mask and smiled at Ali. "Sorry, honey," she said. "I just can't wait for my luxury spa experience."

"Oof!" Ali's dad groaned. He was sitting cross-legged on the floor and looked as if he was in lots of pain. "Check this out." He waved the brochure with *Joseph West's Relaxation Retreat* printed on it in gold letters. "This says that after two days with them, I could be so good at yoga, I'd be able to wrap my legs around my neck."

Ali tried to picture that. Ouch!

"Well, I've just tried it," her dad went on,

"and the only way I'll be able to wrap my legs around my neck is if I cut them off!"

"Think positive!" Gran said, taking the brochure. Ali's grandmother was spending the night with them. Tomorrow, they would leave for Joseph West's. Gran began to leaf through the glossy pages. "I wonder if there are any good antique stores nearby."

Ali's mom shook her head. "Shopping isn't relaxing," she pointed out. "Especially not junk shopping."

"But Gran buys *great* stuff," Ali said loyally. She'd nicknamed her gran the Junk Queen because of her passion for garage sales. It was Gran who'd bought the old Lava lamp that held Little Genie at a flea market. But none of the family, not even Gran, knew that Ali had a real live genie hidden away in her bedroom!

"What's so great about relaxing, anyway?" grumbled Jake, tossing his soccer ball from one hand to the other. "Relaxing's *boring*. Anyway, I can relax like *this*!" And he dropped the ball on the floor and gave it a good kick before their dad grabbed him and started wrestling.

Ali rolled her eyes and headed back upstairs. She couldn't even concentrate on watching *Stay or Go*. She had her own problems to figure out. Like what to do with Little Genie while they were away.

Ali always felt a little nervous leaving Little Genie alone. Genie had been expelled from Genie School. Her teachers had sent her to live in the Lava lamp way back in 1964 so that she could spend some time improving her magic skills. Ali knew Little Genie meant well, but sometimes her magic didn't work out the way she intended. That was why Ali didn't want to take Little Genie with them. *Anything* might happen.

Ali opened her bedroom door and went in. To her surprise, the stuffed animals she usually kept on her bed were floating around the room like astronauts in space.

"Genie!" Ali exclaimed with a grin, dodging a teddy bear as it drifted past her cheek. "What are you *doing?*"

Genie waved at Ali from the desk. She was sitting on the edge, swinging her legs in her sparkly purple pants. "I'm getting to know Herbert and Molly," she explained, pointing to a furry blue hippo and a stray dolphin. "After all, they'll be the only friends I have left when you've gone away on vacation."

Ali felt nervous all over again. "You *are*

going to behave while we're away, aren't you?" she asked.

Little Genie looked indignant. "Behave?" she echoed. "Of *course* I'm going to behave! Don't I always? And I'll have plenty to do while you're gone. I have plans!"

"What plans?" Ali wanted to know.

"Well, I noticed some of the rooms downstairs are looking kind of shabby," Genie went on. "They could do with a little groovy redecoration. But I don't want to say too much. It'll spoil the surprise!"

Uh-oh, Ali thought. Not long ago, she had used one of her wishes to redecorate her bedroom in pink. But Genie's magic had made everything Ali touched pink, including Mary's brother's soccer uniform!

"I'm going to be *sooo* lonely while you're

away." Genie slumped down on the desk with a loud sigh. Even her bouncy blond ponytail was drooping. "But don't worry about little old me. I'll entertain myself *somehow!*"

"That's what I'm afraid of!" Ali murmured, trying not to smile. She began to reconsider. If Little Genie came with them, Ali would be able to keep an eye on her. And she *loved* having Genie around—it made life much more fun and exciting.

Stay or go? It was just like Ali's favorite show. Ali made a decision. "Okay, Genie, you can come with us."

"Far out!" Genie jumped to her feet. Her sparkly purple pants billowed around her as she high-kicked her way across the desk, the curly toes of her golden slippers

almost touching her ponytail. "I'm going on vacation, woo-hoo! Hurry and pack my lamp, Ali!"

"Your lamp?" Ali repeated. "You're kidding, aren't you?" She glanced over at the large pink Lava lamp. "Genie, I don't have room in my suitcase for it. Besides, everyone will think I'm *crazy* taking my Lava lamp on a trip!"

Genie stopped high-kicking and slumped down on the desk again. "I can't go anywhere without my lamp," she said miserably. "So I'll have to stay here. I'm going to be *sooo* unhappy when you go away and leave me all by my little lonesome...."

Ali rolled her eyes. "Okay, okay! The lamp can come too." She picked it up from the desk. "I'll have to take something else out of my suitcase, though." Ali's dad had lined the suitcases up by the door downstairs.

Genie's smile stretched from ear to ear.

"This is going to be great! I really need a spa vacation. It's hard work making all your wishes come true, you know, Ali."

Ali peeked at the hourglass-shaped gold watch on Genie's wrist. The top half of the hourglass was full of pink sand, and every time the grains began to trickle through to the bottom, Ali got three wishes. At the moment, though, the sand wasn't moving. Neither Ali nor Genie ever knew when it was going to start.

Genie pulled some paper clips and rubber bands from Ali's desk tray and attached them to a square piece of notepaper. "Wheee!" she shouted, launching herself off the desk with her homemade parachute. She floated gently downward and straight into the open top of Ali's backpack. Ali couldn't help laughing. "I'll see you mañana," Genie announced from inside the backpack. "I can't wait for my de-stressing massage!"

* * *

"Time to go, Ali!" her mom called the next morning.

"Coming!" Ali said. She wrapped the Lava lamp in a sweatshirt, then peeked in the backpack. Little Genie was wearing a pair of yoga pants and a pink leotard. She gave Ali a thumbs-up.

"Okay, Genie. Here we go!" Ali slung her backpack over her shoulder and hurried out to peer over the banister. She didn't want anyone to see her put the lamp in her suitcase. Luckily, her parents and Gran were busy packing the minivan, and Jake was outside too, getting in the way as usual.

Ali rushed downstairs and opened her

suitcase. She'd have to take something out to fit the lamp in. Something that took up a lot of room. She rummaged around for a moment, pulled out a thick sweater, shoved the lamp into the suitcase, and zipped it shut.

Just then, her mom came in. "If you wheel your suitcase to the car, we'll be ready to go."

"Okay, Mom!" Ali *was* looking forward to relaxing at the spa now. And Genie *had* been working very hard granting Ali's wishes. Her tiny friend really did deserve a break, along with the rest of the family.

Joseph West's Relaxation Retreat was three hours away. Ali brought a mystery novel for the ride. But every few pages, she peeked into her backpack to check on

Genie. Genie had her eyes closed, and she looked like she was doing a yoga chant. It was all Ali could do not to giggle.

As usual, the only thing annoying Ali was Jake. He couldn't sit still for five minutes.

"Jake," Ali groaned as they drove along the highway, "I've asked you to stop kicking the back of my seat a hundred times!"

"Thirty-two times, actually," Jake replied from the back as he continued to kick Ali's seat hard.

Ali gritted her teeth. Gran, who was sitting next to her, was dozing and listening to her MP3 player. With her eyes shut, Gran couldn't hear a thing as she tapped her toes in time to the music. Ali wished she'd brought some music to listen to as well, instead of being stuck with Bulldozer's lame jokes and her mom and dad's debates about what activities they were going to do at the spa.

"Okay, so you're not interested in tree meditation or a hot stone massage," Mrs. Miller said, flipping through the brochure. "What about ear candles?"

"No one's putting a candle in my ear, thank you very much!" Mr. Miller exclaimed in horror. Ali giggled.

"It's supposed to be very relaxing," her mom pointed out.

"Yes, until your hair catches fire!" Ali's dad said. "Isn't there anything *normal* to do in this place?"

"Dad's right, Mom," Ali chimed in. "Ear candles do sound pretty weird." When Ali thought of a spa, she imagined sitting on a lounge chair in the sun drinking fruit smoothies, and splashing around in the pool. Ear candles? Yuck!

"Here." Ali's mom handed her the brochure. "I'm sure you can find something you'll like."

Ali flipped through the pages. There was a lot of stuff about "relaxing and reenergizing," but this didn't exactly fit with the photo of guests trekking uphill with heavy backpacks, not to mention the fact that every morning started with a two-mile jog! She frowned. The Relaxation Retreat looked more like a really tough gym class than a luxury spa. The pool was unheated and for exercise use only, and there wasn't a lounge chair in sight!

"Oh no," Ali groaned. "This isn't what I thought it would be at all. I wish this vacation could be a little more fun!"

Suddenly, Little Genie peered out of Ali's backpack. She checked that Gran was asleep and then turned to Ali. "The sand has started falling through the hourglass!" she whispered, holding out her wrist.

"What?" Ali gasped, looking down at Genie's watch. Sure enough, a small pile of glittering pink granules had started gathering in the bottom half of the hourglass.

"Your wish is going to come true!" Genie beamed at Ali before ducking out of sight again.

"Oh!" Ali gulped as Genie's words sank in. She was going to get her wish for a more fun-filled vacation! But ... this was the first time any of her wishes had involved her family. And who could tell what "more fun" might mean with one of Genie's spells?

Ali couldn't undo any of her wishes. They always lasted until the last grain of pink sand had fallen through the hourglass. And because the hourglass ran on Genie Time—which was very unpredictable—that could be minutes or hours. Or days!

Ali felt a quiver of excitement shoot through her.

What had she gotten them all into?

Chapter Three
Welcome to
Cowboy Country

"We turn off here," Ali's mom said a few moments later as she studied the map. "Look, there's a sign up ahead."

They all stared at the big wooden sign. It had two large horseshoes nailed to the sides and was surrounded by cacti.

"This way to Cowboy Joe's Wild West Ranch," Ali read aloud. "Are you sure this is right, Mom?"

Mrs. Miller nodded, looking rather

bewildered. "But it should say Joseph West's Relaxation Retreat!"

"Maybe the place has changed its name?" Gran suggested.

Suddenly, very faintly, Ali heard the sound of singing from inside her backpack.

"I was born under a wanderin' star!"

Then Ali realized what had happened. This was something to do with her wish. Genie's magic must have changed the spa to a Wild West ranch! Ali grinned. A ranch sounded *a lot* more exciting than what was in Mom's brochure.

"You mean we're going to be cowboys?" Jake asked excitedly. He waved his arm over his head, throwing an imaginary lasso. "Yee-haw! Do you think they'll show us how to rope steers? Ali, you pretend to be a steer and I'll rope you!"

"No, you won't," Ali said sternly as Mr. Miller pulled up to the ranch entrance. They drove through wooden gates into a large yard dotted with clumps of cacti and surrounded by log cabins and a paddock full of cattle.

"This isn't what I was expecting," Mrs. Miller said in a dazed voice as they climbed out of the minivan. A young couple on horses trotted past them. Ali saw a family headed off down a path carrying fishing poles and a picnic basket.

Me neither! Ali thought.

"But it sure looks fun!" Ali's dad said.

A genuine-looking cowboy with a wrinkled brown face was making his way across the yard toward them. He wore dusty black jeans, leather boots, a fringed vest, and an enormous black Stetson hat.

"Why, hello," Ali's mom said.

"Howdy, ma'am," the man drawled, tipping his hat to them. "I'm Cowboy Joe."

"I think we're in the wrong place," Mrs. Miller told him. "We're supposed to be going to a spa."

"Ain't no spa here," Cowboy Joe said. "You *are* the Millers, aren't you?"

Ali nodded, along with everyone else.

"Then you're in the right place." Cowboy Joe took a piece of paper from his pocket and checked it. "Three adults and two kids, and you're booked for three days."

"Cool!" Jake said, looking excited.

"One of the boys will wrangle your luggage. So come along with me and I'll show you to your cabin." And Cowboy Joe ambled off.

"What are we going to do?" Mom

wailed. "What about my hot stone massage?"

"We'll just have to make the best of it," Mr. Miller said with a shrug. "I have to say, this looks a lot better than trying to wrap my legs around my neck!"

"I want to learn how to rope a steer," Jake chimed in.

"Howdy, longhorns," Gran said cheerfully, waving at the mooing cattle in the paddock. "Did you know, Ali, that I worked on a ranch in Wyoming one summer before I met your grandpa?" Ali shook her head.

Gran beamed. "Riding horses and sitting around campfires—ah, I remember it well. I'm going to enjoy this!"

Ali couldn't help feeling sorry for her mom, and a little guilty, as they followed Cowboy Joe over to a large log cabin. But her dad was right. This vacation was looking much more exciting, thanks to Genie!

"You're plumb next to this paddock here, so I hope the cattle won't keep you awake," Cowboy Joe said, unlocking the cabin door. "But with all the activities I've got planned for you, you'll be plenty tuckered out anyway!"

"Don't worry," Mr. Miller said. "Any noise is better than the sound of yoga chants."

Cowboy Joe looked puzzled.

"What kind of activities, Cowboy Joe?" Ali asked quickly, before he could start asking questions.

"See those ranch hands?" Cowboy Joe pointed to a couple of men in the paddock. "You're going to learn to do all the things *they* do. Lassoing and herding cattle, cooking over a campfire, riding the mules."

"I'm gonna be the best cowboy ever," Jake boasted. "Yee-haw!"

Ali rolled her eyes.

"You'll be doing some of the activities with other guests and some in your family group," Cowboy Joe went on. "Whenever you do well, you'll earn a horseshoe. And if you have three horseshoes by the end of your stay, you'll win a real-deal Stetson just like mine. Now I'll let you settle in and get changed, folks, while I mosey on back to the big lodge and let Betty in the office know you're here." And he tipped his hat again before he left.

"I really want to get a cowboy hat," Jake said as the Millers walked into the cabin. The floor was made from wide pine planks, and there was a big stone fireplace with plaid couches and an armchair surrounding it. Ali thought it looked very cozy.

"You heard what Cowboy Joe said," Ali reminded him. "You have to earn the horseshoes to get a hat."

Jake stuck out his tongue at her and climbed onto the arm of one of the couches. "Ride 'em, cowboy!" he yelled.

"I wonder how this mix-up happened," Ali's mom murmured with a sigh, looking around the cabin. "I hope we're going to enjoy it here."

"I'm *sure* we will!" Ali told her mom confidently, giving her a hug. Mrs. Miller ran her hand over the checkered quilt on the chair, looking thoughtful.

There was a knock on the door, and Ali spotted another cowboy through the window with their suitcases. "I'll take care of that," Ali's dad said. "I think that's your room, Ali." He pointed to the door with a sign that said LI'L COWGIRL.

Ali went in to explore, and the minute she closed the door, there was a tiny cry of "Giddyup!" from Ali's backpack. Little Genie sprang out. She was wearing a miniature cowgirl outfit with a pink cowboy hat, pink jeans, pink leather chaps, a checked shirt, and pink boots, and carrying a mini-lasso.

"Howdy, pardner!" she yelled.

Chapter Four
Rooping the Wind

"I can't wait to start being a cowgirl!" Genie said. "I'm going to find me a fine, strong cow, saddle it up, and go for a ride. This is the best wish *ever.*"

Ali burst out laughing. "Genie, cowboys don't ride cows!" she said. "They ride *horses.*"

"Oh, right." Genie frowned, looking down at the lasso. "And what's *this* for? Tying up annoying people like Jake?"

Ali giggled. "I think it's for catching stray cattle and bringing them back to the herd."

Genie looked puzzled. "Can't you just ask them nicely not to wander off?"

Ali shook her head. "I can't see that working," she said. "Do you speak cow?"

"I guess not—but I could try!" said Genie. She walked a few strides, listening to the swish of her chaps. "When do I get to rodeo?" she asked hopefully.

"I don't think there's a rodeo here," Ali said. It looked more like a working farm than a place that would put on rodeo shows. "But, well, maybe you'll get the chance to ride a bucking bronco."

"A bucking bronco?" Genie echoed. "Great!" She smoothed the fringes on her chaps. "But ... what *is* a bucking bronco?"

"It's a wild horse," Ali explained. On second thought, Ali hoped that if there were any bucking broncos at the ranch, Genie would stay far away from them. She looked around her room. "Cowboy Joe said we were supposed to get changed. Do you think there's a cowgirl outfit here for me?"

"Try the armoire," suggested Genie.

Ali opened the door. Inside she found a fringed sky blue jacket, leather chaps, and square-toed tan leather boots. A matching bandana completed the outfit.

"I think I'm going to like being a cowgirl!" Ali said happily as she changed into the clothes. "I hope I win a Stetson like Cowboy Joe's."

"I wonder if they have pink ones, like mine," Genie said, waving hers around.

Ali giggled. "I don't think pink is Cowboy Joe's color," she said, adjusting her collar.

Genie tapped her boot. "Hurry up, Ali. I want to go explore the ranch!"

"We'll go together," Ali told her. "I'll just unpack your lamp."

On the bedside table there was a large porcelain lamp shaped like a cowboy roping a steer. Ali pushed the Lava lamp out of sight behind it. "Perfect."

"If I'm going out there with you, then I need somewhere to hide," Genie said thoughtfully, looking at Ali's outfit. "Got it!" She snapped her fingers. There was a puff of pink smoke and a sky blue pistol holster appeared around Ali's waist.

The pistol holster was perfectly Genie sized. Ali carefully helped Genie inside and, making sure Little Genie was out of sight, went out into the living room.

"Yee-haw, pardner!" Gran waved at Ali. "You look mighty fine!"

"So do you, Gran," Ali replied with a grin. Her gran looked so different—and very chic—in her fringed white cowgirl outfit.

"Out of my way!" Jake yelled, jostling past Ali and Gran. He wore jeans and a blue and red cowboy shirt. "I'm chasing a runaway steer!" And he galloped off into the kitchen.

"What do you think?" Ali's dad came out of the bedroom, adjusting his bolero. He wore a checked shirt and jeans like Jake's.

"You look great," Gran assured him.

"How's Mom?" Ali asked. She still felt guilty for wishing away her mom's spa vacation.

Before Ali's dad could answer, her mother hurried out of the bedroom. She wore the exact same outfit as Ali, except hers was dark blue. Ali was relieved to see she was smiling.

"I think I'm going to enjoy this, now that I've gotten over the shock," her mom said. "This will be a real family vacation. We'll be outdoors all day, bonding with nature. And I can't wait to try cooking over a campfire!"

Ali felt relieved. For once, it looked like one of her wishes was completely problem free!

"I'm a Texas ranger and I'm coming to catch the cattle rustlers!" Jake shouted, zooming back into the living room. He flopped onto the couch, panting. "Wouldn't it be cool if there really were some cattle rustlers? Then the rangers would come and there'd be a shoot-out!"

There was a knock at the door. Gran opened it.

"Howdy, folks." A young man with dark hair stood outside. "I'm Tim, one of the cowhands here at the ranch." He was dressed in a spotless cowboy outfit with shiny silver spurs, and he carried a large lasso.

"It's time for your first activity," Tim said, blinking a little at the sight of Gran in her dazzling white cowgirl outfit. "Practicing lassoing. I have some lassos outside for you."

"You were right, Ali," her mom whispered as they all trooped out into the yard. "This is going to be fun!"

"Now, don't get too downhearted if

you're not very good," Tim said, handing out coils of rope. "No one is, at first." He puffed out his chest. "I've been roping for a long, long time."

Ali glanced down to see Genie peeking out of the pistol holster. She was rolling her eyes. Tim obviously took his "roping" very seriously!

They began by throwing the ropes onto the ground to get the kinks out. Then Tim showed them how to tie a noose at one end and coil the lasso up again, ready to be thrown. From the movements Ali could feel in her pistol holster, she guessed that Genie was doing the same with her miniature lasso.

"Are we going to rope some cattle now?" Jake asked after Tim taught them how to swing the lasso overhead and let it go.

Tim shook his head. He pointed to a big clump of cacti in the middle of the yard. "We'll begin by trying to lasso something that isn't moving. Pick a cactus and try to rope it."

"Me first!" Jake shouted. He waved the lasso enthusiastically and flung it at his chosen cactus. The noose fell to the ground two or three feet away.

Mr. Miller and Gran went next, but although Ali's dad got close, neither of them was able to rope their cactus. Then it was Ali's turn. She chose a short, stumpy cactus with a furry top and stepped forward. She tried to do exactly what Tim had shown them. But timing exactly when to let go of the rope was tricky! The coils flew out of her hand and the noose ended up even farther away from her cactus than Jake's and Gran's had been from theirs.

"Ali's terrible!" Jake shouted gleefully.

"Don't worry, Ali," Tim said, motioning for Mrs. Miller to take her turn. "Beginners can barely rope a cactus during the first lesson. Like I said before, it takes time to become as good at lassoing as I am." He stopped in amazement as Ali's mom threw her lasso and the noose fell neatly around her cactus.

"Way to go, Mom!" Ali cried as the rest of the family broke into cheers.

"That's what happens when you learn from a pro," Tim said approvingly. "Let's see if the rest of you can do that."

Mr. Miller stepped up first, but this time

his aim was way off target. So were Gran's and Jake's. Taking a deep breath, Ali tried again but ended up almost lassoing Cowboy Joe, who was strolling across the yard.

Tim let out a big sigh. "People, people. You're not remembering what I told you." Tim picked up a spare lasso and began coiling it expertly. "Watch me. I'll rope Ali's cactus and show you *exactly* how to do it."

"Ali!" Ali heard a tiny, muffled whisper from her holster. She moved away from the others. She didn't want to look stupid staring down at her hip and talking to her holster! "He's such a show-off!" Little Genie said. "I think he needs to be taught a lesson!"

And before Ali could say anything, Genie

snapped her fingers. A wisp of sparkly pink smoke drifted toward Ali's cactus. As Ali watched in amazement, the spiky green plant gave a tiny twitch, nodded its furry head, and *shuffled* farther away across the yard. Alarmed, Ali glanced at her family, but they were busy watching Tim coil his lasso, and Tim was facing the other way.

"Now," Tim announced as he waved the lasso over his head, "watch how a *real* cowboy does it!" He spun around and hurled the rope spectacularly toward the place where Ali's cactus had been. But thanks to Little Genie's magic, there was nothing there. The lasso fell to the ground, empty.

"You missed!" Jake said excitedly.

"What?" Tim burst out. "That's never

happened before. It was almost like the cactus moved out of the way!"

Gran chuckled. "It looks like even pros make mistakes."

"Why don't you try again, Ali?" Mom said.

"Yes, go on, Ali," whispered Genie from

the holster. "Quick, while everyone else is coiling up their ropes!"

Ali stepped forward and threw her lasso. Immediately her little cactus dashed toward the noose. It ducked its furry head inside and came to a full stop as the rope fell neatly around it.

"I did it!" Ali yelled, punching the air with her fist.

Everyone turned to look.

"Great job, honey!" called Mom.

"I hate to burst your bubble, but that doesn't count," Tim said, shaking his head. "You need to rope your own cactus, not someone else's." He pointed at the cacti. "That's not *your* cactus. It just looks the same, that's all."

Ali sighed. She *had* roped a cactus— with a little magical help!

"Don't worry, Ali," whispered Genie, peeking out of the holster. "There'll be plenty of things here you're good at!"

Ali watched as Tim stomped out to the cacti to retrieve the lassos. Making friends with him was definitely not one of them!

Chapter Five
A Talkative New Friend

At lunch in the ranch canteen, Ali and her family met several of the other guests, who were very friendly. No one else seemed surprised that they were at a ranch instead of a spa. Ali wondered if Genie's magic had affected their vacation destinations too. *Or maybe they had* planned *on coming to a ranch,* Ali said to herself, taking a big bite of her chili dog. Either way, it was too late now to do anything but sit back and enjoy the trip.

When they'd finished eating, Cowboy Joe banged his spoon on his tin mug to get their attention.

"All right, pardners," he drawled. "Now that we're done breaking bread together, this afternoon we're all going on a mule ride. There's all sorts of trails to keep you folks busy, and acres of wilderness just waiting to be seen. So let's get going!"

There was a buzz of excitement as everyone trooped out of the canteen and into the yard. *A mule ride sounds like fun,* Ali thought. And maybe she'd get her first horseshoe!

"Groovy!" Little Genie whispered from Ali's holster. "A mule ride!"

The mules were tied to the paddock fence, and Cowboy Joe introduced each guest to their animal. Ali was really excited as she waited her turn. She'd never seen a live mule before. Some of the mules were gray, while others were brown or black. They had long ears and short manes.

"This is Trigger," Cowboy Joe said, leading Ali over to a gray mule with four white-socked legs.

Ali patted Trigger on the nose as Genie, making sure no one was watching, popped up out of the holster and stroked his mane. The mule sniffed curiously at Genie's ponytail.

Ali smiled. "I think you've made a new friend, Genie!" she whispered.

Cowboy Joe showed everyone how to saddle up, and then all the guests had to do it themselves. It looked easy, but Ali soon found out that it wasn't. The leather saddles were very heavy and hard to lift onto the mule's back. There was one large strap that fastened under the mule's stomach and two smaller straps to keep the saddle in place.

Ali was soon frustrated as she tried to work out which strap went where. She glanced over at the rest of her family. Her dad, who had learned to ride when he was a kid, was already saddled up and ready to go. Her mom was helping Jake. Even Gran looked almost ready to ride.

Suddenly there was a shout of laughter from Jake. "Ali's put her saddle on back to front!"

Ali looked down at the saddle. Maybe that was why she was having such a hard time. "Oops," she said, feeling embarrassed.

Even worse, Trigger was staring right at her, and Ali was convinced that the mule was rolling his eyes!

"Easy mistake to make," Cowboy Joe said kindly, ambling over to help.

Once all the mules were saddled up, everybody climbed on.

"I feel like I'm in a western movie!" Ali's dad said. "I wonder if I could get away with wearing this outfit back home?"

"Don't you dare," Ali warned, then laughed as her dad winked at her.

"Let's go!" Cowboy Joe shouted. "Giddyup!"

"Giddyup, Trigger," Ali said, tapping her heels lightly against the mule's sides. He didn't move.

"Giddyup!" Ali said more loudly as the other mules began trotting around her to follow Cowboy Joe. But still Trigger didn't budge.

"Ali's stuck!" Jake yelled, riding his mule, Walker, in a circle around Ali and Trigger before heading after the others.

"Go on without me," Ali called as Cowboy Joe turned to look. "I'll catch up." Somehow she had to get Trigger moving!

"What about a carrot to dangle in front of his nose?" Genie suggested, climbing out of the holster and onto the saddle. "I could zap one up."

"No thanks, Genie, I really want to do this myself," Ali said. "Oh, I *wish* Trigger would just listen to me!"

Suddenly a sparkly pink cloud appeared and surrounded them.

Little Genie beamed. "That's your second wish, Ali!"

Ali gasped. She'd forgotten she still had two wishes left!

"Could you start walking, please, Trigger?" she asked politely.

But instead of trotting forward, the mule turned his head to look at her. "No, I can't!" he brayed.

"You ... you can talk!" Ali spluttered. She was very glad there was no one else around in the yard to hear *this*.

"Well, of course. You see," Trigger went on, "I have an itch underneath my saddle blanket. It's an extremely bad itch, and I couldn't possibly walk *anywhere* with an itch like this one."

Ali opened her mouth to say something, but Trigger didn't give her a chance. He sighed loudly. "People just don't understand what it's like for a mule to have to carry things everywhere. And carrying people is *especially* difficult!"

"Sorry," Ali said. It looked like she not only had a talking mule, she had a talking mule with attitude! "This isn't exactly what I had in mind," she whispered to Genie.

"Well," Little Genie whispered back, "you only wished for him to listen, not to do whatever you asked."

"Let me scratch your itch, Trigger," Ali said, hoping this would make the mule happier. "Where is it?"

"On my right side," Trigger directed her. "No, a bit lower down. Now to the left. Yes, there!"

Ali gave the mule a good scratch. Trigger whinnied and then shook his mane. "Well, I suppose we'd better get along, then," he said, and slowly moved off.

Ali was extremely relieved. "I just hope he doesn't start talking when the others are around," she murmured to Genie. "How would I explain *that*?"

Little Genie nodded, looking concerned. Catching hold of Trigger's tufty mane, she scrambled up toward his ears. "Hey, Trigger, how's it going?" she said cheerfully. "By the way, I don't think you should say anything in front of the others. They'll just be jealous that they haven't got a wonderful, clever talking mule like you!"

Trigger nodded. "You're right," he said. "It *is* tough being so wonderful!"

Ali grinned. The sky was blue, the sun was warm on her back, and the air was fresh and piney. She wondered what she'd be doing if the hourglass sand ran out right now, the magic faded away, and she found herself at the spa instead. Taking a "relaxing" mountain hike, or getting twisted up in a yoga pose? A talking mule and a Wild West ranch were much more fun!

Ali noticed her brother up ahead. He was hanging far back from the rest of the group. "Why has Jake stopped?" Ali wondered aloud.

"I bet he's up to something!" Genie said, scampering back into the holster. "Let's go find out."

Trigger sighed again. "Excuse me, but I've only just got going," he whinnied.

"Won't it be nice to have a rest for a few minutes?" Ali said. "You can stop when we catch up with Walker."

"Hmph," Trigger said. "I *do* find it quite

annoying when people keep stopping and starting!" But the mule stopped when they reached Jake and his mule.

Jake was leaning out of the saddle, examining the ground near one of the paddock fences.

"What are you doing, Jake?" Ali asked.

"Look." Jake pointed down at the dusty ground. There was a mass of footprints right next to the fence. "Someone's been standing here watching the cows. I bet there are rustlers coming after Cowboy Joe's longhorns!"

Ali shook her head. Jake was being ridiculous—again! "There are lots of workers around the ranch," she reminded him. "*They* probably made the footprints."

Jake made a face at her. "These are

definitely the mark of cattle rustlers!" he insisted, gathering up Walker's reins and trotting off.

"Ooh, rustlers!" Little Genie gazed excitedly up at Ali from the holster. "Look, there are some broken branches on that tree there. Do you think the rustlers climbed it to check out the lay of the land?"

"No," Ali said firmly. "Honestly, Genie, you're as bad as Jake! Giddyup, Trigger!"

Trigger muttered something under his breath but trotted after Jake. As they followed Walker along the trail, Ali noticed something ahead of her, wriggling out of the undergrowth. She gasped as she saw a long black snake slither across the trail right in front of Jake's mule.

Walker leapt away from the snake in

alarm. He let out a deafening whinny and dashed off along the trail at high speed, with Jake clinging on for dear life.

"Walker's been spooked by a snake!" Ali cried. "Genie, what are we going to do?"

Chapter Six
Racing to the Rescue

"Help!" Jake shouted as Walker flew along the dusty trail.

"Bulldozer!" Ali cried.

"Don't be scared, Ali," Genie yelled, jumping out of the holster as Trigger followed the runaway mule at a slower pace. "Leave this to me!"

Balancing on Trigger's back, Little Genie snapped her fingers, and a magic lasso appeared in a rush of pink sparkles. Ali could see that Jake was still holding on to Walker's reins. His bandana had fallen over his face.

"Yee-haw!" Genie shouted, circling the lasso above her. She let it fly and the rope zoomed through the air and slipped over Walker's head as he raced on.

"See, I told you to leave it to me!" Genie called out. But instead of being able to use the rope to slow Walker down, Genie was whipped from Trigger's back and went flying through the air, clinging to the rope as it flew behind the galloping mule.

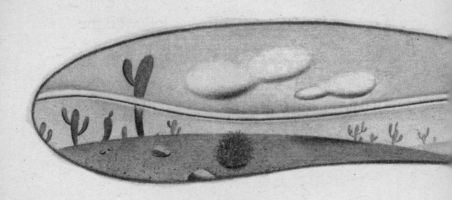

"Genie's being dragged along behind Jake and Walker!" Ali gasped as she urged her mule after them. "We've got to do something, Trigger!"

"Like what?" Trigger demanded.

"Maybe we can catch them!" Ali said desperately. "Can't you go any faster?"

"Faster!" Trigger repeated in an offended tone. "Of *course* I can go faster. I'm much quicker than Walker. Once we had a race and I—"

"That's great, Trigger. Why don't you

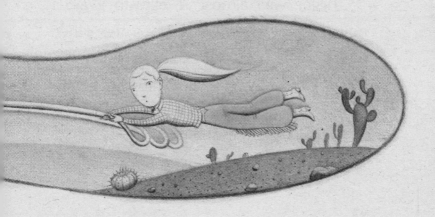

show me?" Ali interrupted him. "Come on! Giddyup!"

"Okeydoke," Trigger said, and hurtled after Jake, Walker, and Genie. Ali was relieved to see that Trigger *was* faster than Walker. Her heart pounded as they galloped closer and closer.

"Hang on!" Ali yelled as she rode past the end of the flying lasso.

"I will!" Genie gasped, her ponytail flying straight out behind her in the wind. "I'm good at hanging on!"

Trigger was almost level with Walker now. Leaning over, Ali grabbed the other mule's reins and was able to slow him down. "It's okay, Walker," she said gently. "Shhh, calm down."

Panting, Walker slowed down some more and then stopped. Little Genie jumped onto Trigger's saddle, thrust the lasso at Ali, and disappeared into the holster just as Jake pushed his bandana off his face.

"Ali?" Jake stared at the rope in her hands with wide eyes. "You lassoed Walker and saved me! You're a real cowgirl now!"

"Um ... that's not exactly how it was ...," Ali began.

But Jake wasn't listening.

By this time the rest of the group had realized that something was wrong and were riding back.

"Cowgirl Ali saved me!" Jake declared. "Walker bolted and she lassoed him!"

"Are you two all right?" their mom asked anxiously as Cowboy Joe dismounted from his own mule and quickly checked Walker over.

"Way to go, Ali!" Mr. Miller said, looking

very proud. Ali blushed as the rest of the group applauded.

"No damage done." Cowboy Joe patted Walker's flank and turned to Ali. "That was a mighty fine thing to do," he said approvingly. "You'll get a horseshoe for that, and so will your brother for not panicking when Walker bolted."

"Yippee!" Jake hollered. "One down, two to go!"

"Your first horseshoe, Ali!" Gran leaned over from her mule and gave Ali a big

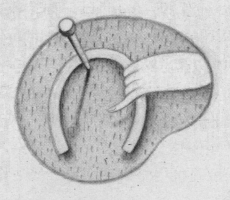

hug, almost toppling over. "You're a really brave girl."

Ali felt a little embarrassed. She hadn't actually lassoed Walker at all; Little Genie and Trigger had done all the hard work.

"But you *did* stop him," Little Genie whispered as they started off down the trail again with Trigger bringing up the rear. It was as if Genie had read her mind. "So you *do* deserve your horseshoe."

"Genie, could you get me a treat for Trigger?" Ali whispered.

With a quick snap of Genie's fingers, a ripe red apple appeared in Ali's hand.

"Thanks very much," said Trigger as Ali dismounted and offered it to him. "It is nice to be appreciated, you know!"

Ali grinned. Trigger might be a bit snappish, but she'd discovered that her

sassy mule had a good heart. Even better,
Jake thought she was the best sister and
cowgirl in the whole world, *and* she had
her first horseshoe.

This was turning into an excellent vacation, thanks to Genie's magic!

*   *   *

"More beans, Ali?" Mom asked, lifting the ladle from the kettle.

Ali nodded and held out her plate. A group of ranch hands had cooked sausages and beans over the campfire, and now everyone was eating under the night sky. Ali gazed up at the huge expanse of deep black above them. She could see lots more glittering silver stars than she could in Cocoa Beach. And even though the night air was cold, the campfire was keeping everyone warm. Ali gave a contented sigh as she slipped a tiny piece of corn bread to Genie to nibble on. Little Genie was snug in Ali's denim jacket pocket.

"Time for some cowboy songs," Cowboy Joe said, taking out his harmonica. "Any volunteers want to accompany me on guitar?"

Gran raised her hand. "I remember many songs from my ranch days!" she told the crowd. "Hopefully I'm not too rusty!"

One of the ranch hands produced a guitar for Gran, and she and Cowboy Joe began to play.

"Oh, give me a home where the buffalo roam," Gran sang. "Join in, everybody!"

Ali didn't know all the words. So she hummed along and sang the chorus.

"Home, home on the range,
Where the deer and the antelope play,
Where seldom is heard a discouraging word
And the skies are not cloudy all day."

*   *   *

As Ali sang along, she could hear Genie singing too. *What a great wish this is!* Ali thought happily, noticing her mom smiling as Cowboy Joe and Gran launched into "Clementine." *I'm so glad we didn't go to the spa, and it looks like Mom feels that way too....*

When they finally went to bed, Ali was feeling very tired. She fell asleep almost immediately. But she was woken up a few hours later by some faint but very strange sounds.

"What's that?" Ali wondered, yawning. She sat up to investigate. There was Genie, sitting on the nightstand, strumming a tiny guitar made of twigs and bits of thread. Moonlight cast a spotlight on her.

"Oh, give me a Lava lamp in the middle of camp," Genie sang.

Ali smiled as she pulled the covers back over herself and closed her eyes. Ali wasn't the only real cowgirl in the Millers' cabin!

Chapter Seven
Breakfast Disaster

"Ah, another beautiful day!" Ali's dad declared, breathing in deeply as the family left their cabin and made their way over to the canteen for breakfast the following morning. "I wonder what cowboy activities we'll be doing today."

"And I've only got two horseshoes left to earn after Cowboy Joe gave me one for my singing last night," Gran said. "I can't wait to get my very own Stetson."

"I'm going to win another horseshoe today!" Jake said.

"I hope I win one too," Ali whispered to Genie—who was back in her holster—as they went into the canteen.

"You will!" Genie whispered back. "Don't worry, I'll help you."

"That's what I'm afraid of!" Ali winked at Genie, who giggled.

"There's still plenty of sand to run through the hourglass," Genie said, holding out her watch to Ali. "Don't forget you've got one wish left."

Ali got in line and picked up her tray. The delicious smells of maple syrup and cinnamon filled the air.

"How about some oatmeal, Ali?" Gran said, pointing to a steaming metal kettle as she moved down the line. "They've got bananas and strawberries to put on top."

"Yum," Ali said. As she began to ladle oatmeal into her bowl, Genie popped up out of the holster again.

"I want some cowboy grub too," she said, holding up a thimble. Before Ali could stop her, Genie leaned out of the holster to scoop up some oatmeal. All of a sudden, the holster flipped forward. Genie tumbled out—right into the oatmeal!

"Help!" Genie spluttered.

Ali had to bite her lip to keep from screaming. Luckily, her family had found a table to sit at, and everyone else in line was paying attention to their food, not to Ali.

Ali pushed up her sleeve, then stuck her

arm into the kettle to fish Genie out. The oatmeal was superhot!

"Young lady!" a stern voice called out.

Ali jumped and turned to see an older woman wearing a hairnet striding toward her. She looked very annoyed. "What are you doing sticking your hands in everyone's breakfast?" she demanded.

"I—uh—" Ali stammered. She couldn't think of anything to say. What if the woman saw Little Genie? Genie would lose her magic powers and be shut up in her lamp forever!

As the woman came closer, Ali stood right in front of the kettle, trying to shield it from view. The woman stepped to the left to get around her, but Ali stepped to the left too and blocked her path. The woman stepped to the right. So did Ali. She had to stop that woman from getting near the kettle!

The woman frowned. "Are you blocking my way?"

"Um, well, not exactly," Ali said.

Finally, the woman nudged Ali aside and

bent over the oatmeal. "Hey! There's something in here!"

Ali's heart pounded with fear. *She's seen her! Does that mean Little Genie has lost all her magic?*

The woman took the ladle and scooped Genie out. Ali saw that Genie was lying perfectly still on the ladle, not moving a muscle. *Oh no! Has Little Genie been cooked?*

"Is this your *doll,* young lady?" the woman asked sternly.

Jake had come up to grab a muffin. He walked over to see what was going on.

"You dropped your doll in the oatmeal, Ali?" Jake asked, taking a bite of his muffin. Crumbs fell onto the floor. "Classic!"

"Yes, she's mine, ma'am," Ali told the woman. She could feel her cheeks turn red.

But it was the only way she could get Genie back!

"Well, here she is." The woman gingerly handed Genie, who was covered in oatmeal, over to Ali. "And be more careful next time. We're going to have to make an entire new batch of oatmeal now."

"I'm very sorry!" Feeling totally flustered, Ali grabbed a couple of paper napkins and cleaned Genie up in a corner where no one could see. *I never should have brought her with us on vacation,* Ali thought miserably.

"Genie!" Ali whispered. Little Genie still hadn't moved. Had Ali lost her best friend? "Genie, please wake up!"

Just when Ali thought Little Genie would never say "groovy" again, Genie opened one eye. "Is it safe?" she whispered.

"Oh, Genie!" Ali held her tiny friend close. "You're okay!"

"Of course I am!" Genie gasped, shaking a lump of oatmeal out of her ear. "I was still as could be, just pretending to be a doll. As long as no humans saw me in action, I'm okay. But it's nice to know you care."

"I'm so glad you aren't cooked!" Ali said. "And if you want some oatmeal, you can share mine." She picked up her bowl and spoon again.

"I don't think so." Little Genie made a face. "I've had enough, thank you!"

*　　*　　*

The day's morning activity was lassoing.

"Cool!" said Jake.

"Again?" Ali said, sighing. Even worse, Tim was their instructor.

Tim pointed to a large metal horseshoe

nailed to one of the paddock fences so that the two ends stuck up in the air. "If you can lasso one of the horseshoe prongs, you get a horseshoe," he explained. He folded his arms. "Go ahead and see how you do. You get three chances."

Everyone had a turn and everyone missed.

"It's not as easy as it looks," Tim said.

"Who said it looked easy?" Ali grumbled.

Ali watched as her dad stepped up for his second try. This time the loop of his lasso headed straight toward the horseshoe, falling neatly over the left-hand prong.

"Dad's done it!" Jake shouted. "Me next!"

Jake, Gran, and Ali had another try, but they all missed again. Then it was Mrs. Miller's turn. Ali held her breath as the rope flew through the air—and lassoed *both* prongs of the horseshoe.

"Mom, you get two horseshoes!" Jake yelled excitedly. "Will you give me one of them?"

"She *hasn't* got two horseshoes," Tim said, looking annoyed. "You can only win *one* horseshoe for this game."

"But she got both prongs at the same time," Ali pointed out. "She should get *two* horseshoes."

"It's against the rules, but I suppose we can make an exception," Tim said, looking less than thrilled.

Jake dashed forward to take his final throw. This time he was able to rope the right-hand prong.

"Yippee!" Jake jumped up and down. "I've won my second horseshoe!"

"Oh, we'll never hear the end of this now," Ali groaned to her gran.

"Quiet, Ali," Gran replied, waving her lasso overhead. "You're distracting me."

Everyone applauded as Gran's rope slipped over the right-hand prong like Jake's had. Ali's heart sank a little. Now she was the only one without a horseshoe for this activity.

"Good luck, Ali!" Genie whispered as the rest of the family gathered around Tim. He'd taken a scorecard from his pocket and was jotting down the number of horseshoes they'd won.

"Thanks!" Ali whispered back, aiming the lasso as carefully as she could. "I really hope I can—"

But before Ali could get the rest of the sentence out, she saw Little Genie leap out of the holster. Genie whizzed through the air and grabbed the loop just as it flew toward the horseshoe.

"I'll help you, Ali!" Genie called as she zoomed straight toward the horse-shoe, clinging tightly to the rope. "I'll make sure the rope goes over one of the prongs!"

To Ali's horror, she suddenly realized that this was her most accurate throw so far and, if she didn't do something fast, Genie would be squished against the giant metal horseshoe!

Immediately, Ali jerked her rope aside, making sure the lasso didn't get anywhere near the prongs. It fell to the ground and Genie bounced into a tumbleweed.

"Nice try, sweetie!" her mom told her. "You were really close that time."

"That's a typical beginner's mistake, jerking the rope like that," Tim said. "Be more careful next time!"

Ali felt even more frustrated as she followed the rope, coiling it as she went along. She scooped up Little Genie, who looked dazed, and put her back into the holster.

"Sorry, Ali!" Genie whispered, pulling a piece of hay from her ponytail.

"Ali's the only one without a horseshoe today," Tim announced, looking up from his scorecard.

Did he have to announce it? Ali thought. Maybe she could think up a good third wish to use on him! But suddenly and un-expectedly, a loop of rope flew past Ali and over Tim's head. It slipped down around his shoulders, pinning his arms to his sides.

"Hey!" Tim yelped at Ali's mom, who held the other end of the lasso. "What are you doing?"

"Sorry," Mrs. Miller said innocently. "It was an accident. I was just trying to rope the horseshoe again." She winked at Ali, making it clear that it hadn't been an accident.

"I'm going to get my Stetson before Ali does!" Jake boasted as they headed off for lunch. "You know what? I bet Ali doesn't win a cowboy hat at all!"

Ali made a face at her brother's back. The trouble was, he might be right, she thought, feeling glum all over again.

"Way to go, your mom!" Genie whispered.

"That stopped Tim in his tracks! But why the long face, Ali?"

"I'm the only one who didn't get a horseshoe," Ali said, "and Jake's not going to let me forget it."

"Don't worry," Little Genie said. "I'll help you win one of those big hats. You'll see!"

Chapter Eight
Real-Life Rustlers

After lunch Ali's family put their new skills to the test. A group of ranch hands showed them how to move the herd of cattle around the paddock in a group, complete with lots of hooting and hollering. Gran, Mrs. Miller, and Mr. Miller all got horseshoes. Jake missed out because he was too concerned with following more "cattle rustler" clues, and Ali couldn't get Trigger anywhere near the giant reddish-brown longhorns.

As they rode out of the paddock, Trigger was the first mule through the gate. "I'm sorry," he said. "I just don't like longhorns when they all start to run around. They scare me."

"I think they're kind of cute," Little Genie said from her perch in Ali's holster.

Ali patted Trigger's neck. "I understand, Trigger. But the bad thing is that I've missed out on a horseshoe again."

"Keep your holster on, Ali!" Genie said. "We don't go home until tomorrow. And you've still got one wish left."

"But what if the sand runs out before we get home?" Ali asked her.

Genie poked her head out. "Then you'll have to pull this one off yourself, cowgirl!"

* * *

"I don't know what activity we're doing tonight, but I sure hope Jake wins his last horseshoe," Ali said to Genie as she walked to the barn after dinner to visit Trigger. Ali had an apple for the mule in her pocket— and Genie was in her holster. "Otherwise, he'll be whining the whole car ride back home."

"That's true." Genie checked her watch. "You'd better hurry," Genie told her. "You're supposed to meet your parents in the yard in five minutes."

Ali nodded. "I guess I won't win a hat myself now," she said sadly. "We only have one more activity left and I only have one horseshoe, so there's no way I can get three."

Genie cocked her head to one side, her

ponytail bouncing. "Shhh!" she whispered. "I hear someone talking."

Ali listened too, and recognized Tim's voice. He was standing on the other side of the barn, out of sight. Just to be on the safe side, Ali helped Genie tuck her hair back into her holster.

"We'll steal them tonight," Tim was saying.

Steal? Ali clapped her hand to her mouth to smother a gasp.

"We'll wait until after midnight," Tim went on. "Everyone'll be asleep then, including Cowboy Joe. They won't hear a thing!" He laughed. "Then we'll be rich!"

It sounded like Tim was plotting to steal something valuable from Cowboy Joe's ranch that very night!

"Did you hear that, Ali?" Genie whispered, peeking up at Ali.

Before Ali had a chance to reply, she heard footsteps coming around the side of the barn. Quickly, she slipped through the door and waited inside, her heart pounding. She saw Tim hurry past the open door. He was putting his cell phone into his pocket.

"Tim's a thief!" Genie climbed out of the holster, looking very excited. "What are we going to do to stop him, Ali?"

"I don't know," Ali replied. Trigger was staring at them from his pen, so she went over and gave him the apple.

"Ah, thank you," Trigger said with satisfaction. "That looks like a mighty fine apple!" He crunched it up and swallowed it in two bites.

"We've got to do *something,* Ali," Genie went on urgently. "We can't let Tim get away with stealing!"

"Yes, but we don't know *what* he's planning to steal," Ali pointed out.

Trigger's ears pricked up. "Don't worry, girls," he said, licking his lips to get the last bits of apple. "I was scared at first too. I thought Tim was planning to steal us mules, but he isn't."

Ali and Genie turned to stare at Trigger.

"You mean, you *heard* what Tim was saying?" Genie demanded, jumping from Ali's arm onto the top bar of the pen.

Trigger nodded. "Yep, he's been planning it forever," the mule explained. "And he's only going to steal those noisy longhorns. This place will be a lot more peaceful when *they're* gone!"

Ali and Genie stared at each other in dismay.

"Tim's going to steal Cowboy Joe's cattle!" Ali exclaimed.

"Jake was right," Genie said. "There *are* cattle rustlers on this ranch!"

Chapter Nine
A Cow Thief

"We have to stop him!" Ali said. "We'd better tell Cowboy Joe right away."

"But will he believe us?" Genie asked.

"I don't know," Ali said slowly. *Would* anyone believe them? After all, Jake had been talking about cattle rustlers ever since they got to the ranch, and no one had taken him seriously. Ali didn't want everyone to think she was copying Jake!

"We'll have to stop the rustlers ourselves!" Little Genie declared. She snapped her fingers, and with a wisp of pink smoke, a star-shaped silver badge appeared on her cowgirl shirt. Ali bent over to see what it said.

"Sheriff," she read out. "Genie, what do you think you're doing? We can't stop Tim and the rustlers on our own!"

"Sure we can, pardner!" Genie strutted up and down the top bar of Trigger's pen. "We'll save those longhorns if it's the last thing we do."

Trigger looked puzzled. "You mean you don't *want* those noisy longhorns to be stolen?" he said. "How strange!"

"I know what we'll do," Genie went on, still pacing. "We'll rope Tim and we'll hog-tie him. Then we'll take him to Cowboy Joe and *make* him confess!"

"Hog-tie?" Ali repeated.

"That's when cowboys tie up the roped cattle with a piggin' string," Trigger explained helpfully. "A piggin' string is a short piece of rope."

"Genie, as much as I would like to, we are *not* going to hog-tie Tim." Ali frowned, thinking hard. "We have to catch him and his buddies in the act, and make sure we have witnesses. We'll sneak out tonight and keep watch when everyone's asleep!" Ali knew her parents would never approve of such a thing—but they didn't know that she had her own genie to keep her safe.

"Yee-haw!" Genie yelled loudly, making Trigger jump. "Me and my deputy Ali are gonna stop those darned rustlers!"

"Could you please stop shouting?" Trigger neighed.

"Tim's going to find out that this ranch ain't big enough for the three of us!" Genie vowed.

Ali couldn't help smiling at Little Genie's determination, even though she secretly felt very nervous. Could they *really* stop the rustlers tonight and save Cowboy Joe's cattle?

* * *

Ali opened her eyes, yawning. She'd been having an awesome dream about lassoing the biggest longhorn on the ranch and earning three horseshoes. Just as Cowboy Joe was presenting her with a Stetson, something had gently tickled her nose and woken her up....

A soft pink light filled the room, and Ali realized that Little Genie's Lava lamp was glowing. A large, fluffy white feather was hovering just above Ali's face, but after a few seconds it vanished in a haze of pink sparkles.

"That was my special genie alarm!" Genie explained, popping out of her lamp. She was wearing bright pink and purple striped pajamas and furry purple slippers. "Time to catch those rustlers!"

Both Ali and Genie got dressed in their cowgirl outfits, and Genie took her place in Ali's holster.

"Ready?" Ali whispered, going over to the bedroom door.

"Ready!" Genie announced, giving Ali a thumbs-up.

Ali carefully opened the door. The cabin was silent and dark except for the moonlight coming in through the windows. Everyone was asleep.

Ali crept across the main room, holding her breath, careful not to make a single sound. As she stepped outside and closed the cabin door behind her, she let out a sigh of relief.

"I thought Jake was *never* going to go to sleep!" she whispered to Genie as they made their way across the yard to the barn. "He was so excited after winning his last horseshoe."

The very last activity of the vacation had been horseshoe pitching in the yard, followed by a movie under the stars. Jake, Dad, and Gran had all tied for first place, and received their third horseshoes, and even though Ali had won second place, she still didn't have enough horseshoes to get a cowboy hat. Everyone else would be presented with their hats before leaving the ranch tomorrow.

"And I'm the only person in the family who won't get one," Ali said glumly.

"Don't worry," Genie said. "You've still got one wish left. You could wish for your own cowboy hat!"

"It wouldn't be the same," Ali said, shaking her head.

Trigger was asleep in his pen when Ali and Genie entered the barn. He was snoring loudly, and he only woke up when Genie tickled his nose through the bars with a piece of straw.

"Hey!" Trigger whinnied. "What's going on?"

"We're going to stop the rustlers," Ali said. "And we need your help."

"What?" Trigger flapped his long ears at Ali. "You know I'm scared of cows. And I'm scared of the dark. By the way, I'm scared of rustlers, too!"

"I'll give you the biggest, juiciest apple I

can find if you help us," Ali promised, leading Trigger out of the pen.

"Two apples," Trigger snorted as Ali quickly saddled him up.

"Deal," Ali said. "Now don't make a sound!"

Genie sat on the saddle in front of Ali as they rode out of the barn.

"Let's patrol the paddocks, pardner," suggested Genie. "Them there rustlers must be *somewhere* close by!"

Ali and Genie rode around the outside of the paddocks, looking for anything suspicious. But the night was silent except for the chirping of crickets and an occasional moo, and the ranch seemed calm and peaceful.

"How are we going to get everyone

outside to catch the rustlers in the act?"
Genie mused aloud as they rode along.
"I know! I could blink up a marching
band! That would wake everyone, wouldn't
it, Ali?"

Ali grinned.

"And I can use my quick-freeze spell,"
Genie went on. "That means I can *freeze*
Tim and the rustlers in the act of stealing
the cattle and *unfreeze* them when Cowboy Joe and the others arrive!"

Ali looked impressed. "Can you really do
that, Genie?"

"Well . . ." Genie looked rather embarrassed. "I'm great at *freezing* spells, but not
so great at *unfreezing* ones. Once I acciden-
tally froze my teacher, Miss Sunshine, and I
couldn't unfreeze her for days!"

"Okay. No freezing spells!" Ali said firmly as they hid behind a large clump of tall cacti.

Half an hour later she was beginning to wonder if the rustlers had changed their minds about robbing Cowboy Joe that night. There was no sign of anyone in any of the paddocks.

"I'm tired," Trigger grumbled. "And I'm cold. How much longer do we have to wait around?"

Ali was cold and tired too. She glanced down at Genie, who was trying not to yawn. "Let's go back to bed," Ali said. "It looks like the rustlers aren't coming after all."

Looking much happier, Trigger trotted along the trail, back toward the ranch.

But as they neared the place where Jake had noticed the footprints, Ali froze in the saddle.

Three shadows were bending over the paddock fence!

Chapter Ten
Happy Trails

Ali reined Trigger in behind a nearby tree. "Look, Genie!" she whispered. "It's the rustlers!"

In the dim moonlight Ali could see that Tim was one of three men. They were whispering together, although Ali and Genie couldn't hear what they were saying. Then the men lifted out a large section of the paddock fence and laid it down on the grass. Ali's heart began to thump. It looked like the robbery was really happening, right under their noses!

"What are they doing?" Ali asked as the men hurried over to their horses, which were tethered close by. "They're not leaving, are they?" Then, as the men rode toward the fence gap, she gasped. "They're going to drive the cattle out of the paddock. We have to stop them, Genie!"

"You could lasso them one by one," Genie suggested as the three rustlers rode into the paddock.

"I wasn't great at lassoing," Ali pointed out. "It could take me all night!"

The men were skillfully rounding up the cattle now, and herding them toward the gap in the fence. A few longhorns had already escaped through the gap, and they ran past Ali and along the trail.

"Why don't we go back to the barn and hide?" Trigger said, glancing nervously at the escaped cows.

Ali ignored him. She had to do *something*. Suddenly, a thought popped into her head. "Genie!" she whispered. "I still have one wish left, don't I?"

Genie checked the watch on her wrist. "The sand's still flowing through the hourglass," she announced, beaming at Ali. "So yes, you do!"

Ali thought for a moment. "I wish the men would get rounded up!" she said.

"Ooh, great wish!" Genie exclaimed. "Let's get these darned rustlers penned up like cattle!"

The next moment there was the sound of galloping hooves. The three horses dashed out of the paddock through the gap in the fence, the men bouncing wildly up and down on their backs.

"What's happening?" Ali heard Tim shout. "My horse is out of control!"

"Mine too!" the other men yelled.

The horses rushed down the trail with the men clinging to their backs. When they drew close to Ali's hiding place, the horses stopped, reared up, and dumped their riders on the ground in a heap.

Ali stared in astonishment as a large group of cacti growing by the side of the trail came to life with a twitch and a shiver, just like her fluffy-topped cactus. With a stiff-sounding rustle, they marched toward the men like a prickly green army. They surrounded Tim and the other two men, penning them firmly inside a small circle.

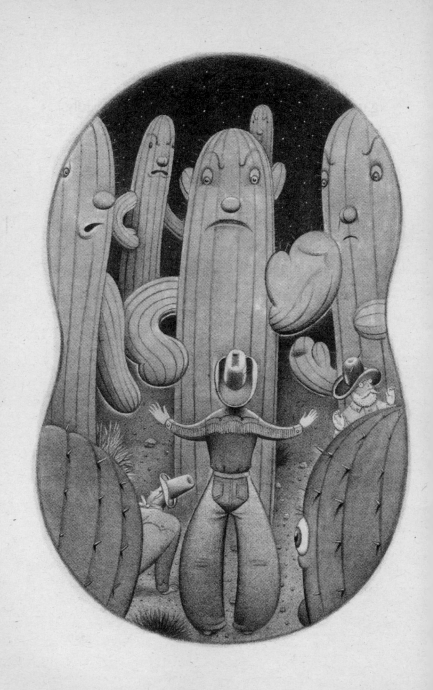

"Owww!" Tim shouted. "I'm getting covered with prickles!"

Little Genie laughed as she scrambled back into the holster. "You'd better raise the alarm, Ali."

Quickly Ali rode into the yard. She jumped off Trigger and ran over to the morning bell, which hung outside the canteen.

Clang! Clang! Clang!

The noise echoed around the yard as Ali rang the bell as hard as she could. Lights went on all over the cabins, and a few moments later, people came rushing outside.

"What's going on?" Cowboy Joe called out. He was wearing bright red long johns and his Stetson.

"Ali!" Mrs. Miller exclaimed as she, Gran,

Jake, and Mr. Miller stumbled sleepily out of their cabin. "Did *you* ring the bell?"

Ali nodded. "I heard noises and I came out to see what was going on, and I found Tim and two other men stealing Cowboy Joe's cattle!" she cried.

"Rustlers!" Jake gasped with excitement. "I knew it!"

Cowboy Joe frowned. "Where are they now?" he asked.

"Over there," Ali replied, pointing in the direction the horses had bolted.

Cowboy Joe and his ranch hands fetched a couple of flashlights and everyone went in search of the rustlers. As they drew near the spot, they could hear loud groans.

"Well, don't that beat all!" Cowboy Joe

burst out laughing as he trained his flashlight on the scene before them. "Looks like these fellas aren't going anywhere!"

Everyone, including Ali and Genie, laughed too as they saw Tim and the other two men caught in the pen of spiky cacti. They were completely hemmed in by the prickly plants and couldn't move an inch.

"Ohhh!" Tim groaned, trying to pull a cactus prickle from his arm. He glared at the other men. "You two are idiots! This is all your fault!"

"I don't know how you three managed to get stuck in there, but you're in big trouble now," Cowboy Joe said, shaking his head. He turned to the ranch hands. "The police are going to be mighty interested in our friends here."

Mrs. Miller took Ali's hands in hers. "I can't believe you've been outside late at night with cattle thieves around!"

"It could have been really dangerous!" her dad said. "Why didn't you tell anyone?"

"I didn't think you'd believe me," Ali said sheepishly.

"Well, it was a brave thing to do, but a silly one!" Ali's mom gave her a hug. "Don't you dare do anything like that again!"

"I promise I won't, Mom. But all I did was ring the bell when I realized what was going on," Ali pointed out. "I didn't really *do* anything else."

Which was true, actually. It was Little Genie and her magic moving cacti that had saved the day!

*　　*　　*

"Gather round the flagpole, folks!" Cowboy Joe called. "It's time for the awards ceremony."

It was the following morning after break-fast, and several families, including the Millers, were packed up and ready to leave the ranch. But first, everyone who'd won three horse-shoes would be presented with their hats.

Ali felt a little sad as she saw the big pile of Stetsons that were to be given out. It looked as if *everyone* had won a hat except her.

"Don't look so down, Ali," Genie whis-pered from inside the holster. "I bet you're the only person here who has their very own genie!"

That made Ali feel better.

"First up, the Miller family. Mrs. Miller!" Cowboy Joe announced.

Ali and the rest of the family cheered as Mrs. Miller went up to receive her cowboy hat, followed by Gran and Mr. Miller. Jake was next, and he looked thrilled when he was given a small black Stetson that fit him perfectly.

"And now we have a special prize," Cowboy Joe said. "This is for a very brave girl who stopped a gang of rustlers from stealing my valuable longhorns." He grinned at Ali. "Come and collect your award!"

Blushing, Ali walked over to him, the cheers of her family and the other guests ringing in her ears. She hadn't expected *this*!

Cowboy Joe held out a shiny pair of silver spurs. "You can wear these on your blue boots," he said as Ali stared at the spurs in delight.

"You mean I can keep the boots?" Ali asked with a grin.

"You sure can. Besides, what else would

you wear with your new hat?" Cowboy Joe
put a Stetson on Ali's head. "Catching those
cattle rustlers is worth fifty horseshoes
to me!"

Ali gasped. "Thank you so much, Cowboy Joe!"

"You're a fantastic cowgirl!" Gran said
proudly, giving her a big hug.

"Great job, Ali," her dad said as the rest
of the family—even Jake—lined up to hug
her too.

After the awards ceremony was over,
Ali and her family went back to their cabin
to change out of their cowboy outfits before leaving for home.

"I get to keep the boots!" Ali said to
Genie, twirling around her bedroom and
admiring the spurs glittering on her heels.

"The spurs are gorgeous." Genie sighed. "I wish I had some."

"Well, we *did* catch the rustlers together," Ali replied. "So you should get some too!" She thought for a moment, and then she opened her suitcase and took out a pair of earrings. Quickly she slipped off the silver backs and attached them to Genie's cowgirl boots.

"My very own spurs!" Genie cried, dancing happily up and down on the bed. "Thanks, Ali."

"I can't believe how well my wishes have worked out," Ali said. "So thank *you*, Genie!" After all that worrying, Ali couldn't have imagined this vacation without her special friend.

"Ali, time to go," her dad called.

Ali and Genie had just enough time to dash to the barn to say goodbye to Trigger and give him the promised two apples before they had to join the rest of the family in the minivan. Cowboy Joe and the ranch hands came to wave them off.

"What a wonderful vacation!" Mom sighed happily as they bumped off down the dusty road. "Even though we weren't at a spa, I feel really relaxed and reenergized."

Suddenly, Ali saw Genie peek out of her backpack, which was on the seat next to her. Genie was waving her wrist madly in the air. The last few grains of sand had fallen through the hourglass, and Ali's wishes were over.

Ali twisted around in her seat. The wooden gates of the ranch had vanished, replaced by ornate, wrought-iron ones below a large white sign with JOSEPH WEST'S RELAXATION RETREAT written on it in gold letters. The herds of cattle had disappeared. The paddocks had been replaced by the swimming pool and exercise studio Ali had seen in the brochure. And instead of log cabins, there were little white clapboard cottages with wind chimes hanging on the verandas. Ali squinted. And was that Cowboy Joe in a yoga leotard?

She breathed a sigh of relief. The spell had lasted just long enough!

Then she noticed that Gran was staring back at the ranch too. She looked extremely puzzled. Ali's heart beat faster as Gran glanced over at her. Genie dove inside the backpack.

"I think I need some new glasses," Gran

muttered, taking hers off and giving them a
good rub on her shirt.

"What was everyone's favorite part
of the vacation?" Ali asked, hoping to
prevent the rest of her family from looking back.

"All of it!" Jake declared.

Mr. and Mrs. Miller nodded.

"I loved it, even though there weren't any antique shops," Gran said.

"We all had such a good time, I think we should come back next year!" Mom declared.

Ali cheered along with Jake and Gran, but inside, her heart sank. *How on earth will I do that?* Meanwhile, Genie was giggling away inside the backpack.

"What about something a bit different for your next family vacation?" Genie whispered. "An astronaut training center? A wilderness survival course? A circus? You could learn how to become a lion tamer, Ali!"

"Nooo!" Ali groaned quietly. "Stop it, Genie!"

Genie winked at her. "Think about it," she whispered. "It'd be fun!"

A *circus* would *be fun,* Ali thought. She'd get to meet all the animals, and she could try bareback riding and acrobatics and the flying trapeze!

Even though Jake began to kick the back of her seat, Ali smiled.

Because life was never, ever boring when you had your very own genie!

About the Author

Miranda Jones lives in a regular house in London. She's sure a genie bottle would be much more exciting.

Don't miss Little Genie #6,
Meanie Genie

When Little Genie's hourglass watch breaks,
leaving Ali the same size as Genie, there's
only one thing for the two friends to do: take
a trip to magical Genieland to ask for help!